SECRETS OF A SUGAR BABY 3

SUGAR BABY SECRETS 3

MIA BLACK

CHAPTER 1

Jae

I stepped into the front room just as the screen flashed the news in front of my eyes. Angie sat with her mouth hanging open as she continued watching the broadcast. I looked at the television screen as the reporter gave more details about the story. "Billionaire playboy Blake Austin has been clearly identified now, but the woman seems to be everything except his wife. Now, for privacy and parental guidance, the recording has been blurred in certain points, but I can tell you this —it is not something that you would want your child to see."

"Turn it off, Angie."

"But Jae—"

"Turn it off!"

She reluctantly grabbed the remote control and switched the channel as I stood dumbfounded in the living room, still trying to piece together what I had just seen. "Did you even know you were being recorded?"

"I didn't know shit, Angie." I plopped down on the couch, still in shell shock of what was going on. *Did Blake record this behind my back and send it out? He wouldn't have done that. He cares about his privacy.* "What the fuck is going on? This shit—this shit is going to ruin everything! They are painting the picture of me being some fuckin' escort! Some whore that sleeps around for money! Erica is going to flip the fuck out!"

"I mean, shit, you know what they say? Any press is good press, you know? Whether it is bad or good. But damn, you be showin' out like that?"

"What?" I looked at her as she typed away on her laptop with her eyes wide open and a smirk clinging to the edge of her lips. "What are you talking about?"

"Shit, you was bussin' it wide open for that nigga. Look at this. It is already on YouTube."

"What?!" I stood up and ran over to her as she sat on the couch so she could show me her screen. The video had been uploaded in a matter of minutes since it replayed over the air, and on there, it was the unedited version. I was bent over on the mattress with my back arched and my ass tooted in the air while he pulled handfuls of my hair at the same time.

"You workin' that nigga, ain't you, Jae?!" she said, laughing.

"This shit is not funny! Take it down!" I said as I furiously pressed buttons on her keyboard. "Take it down! Now!"

"Jae, I didn't put that shit on there, so I can't take it down." She pointed at the screen. "Got damn, look at the views. It's already over 1k and this shit was just put up like five minutes ago."

I leaned back on the couch as she took the laptop away from me. I ran my hands over my face like a wet rag as tears started to form in my eyes. I couldn't believe all of this had happened, but how? Why? Who would do it? There were so many questions that needed answered and I didn't know how to get them. Just then, my phone buzzed in my pocket.

I wiped my eyes dry so I could see the screen clearly. Erica's name popped up. I exhaled and shook my head, knowing that she had seen the news as well. I looked at Angie's laptop just as she spoke. "Damn, YouTube must've snatched that shit down. I can't even look at it no more."

"Why would you want to?"

"Because, bitch, you were showing me some new moves I can use to snatch some of these niggas souls out here. Damn. I didn't know you had it like that, sis."

I rolled my eyes and took a deep breath before I answered my line. "Hello?"

"Jae, I need to see you down at my office immediately."

"Erica, I don't know what—"

"Jae, just come down here. We will talk about the details when you arrive. Can you come now?"

I shook my head again. "Yes, I can come now."

"Good. See you shortly."

I hung up the phone, then slowly pulled myself out of my seat so I could make my way to Erica's office. I prepared myself for the worst news. I knew this wasn't the type of thing she wanted for her business, so in the back of my mind, I had already convinced myself that I wasn't going to be able to work for her anymore.

As soon as I got to the office, Blake stood up and rushed towards me. He wrapped me in his arms as I tied mine around him. "I am glad you were able to come here. I'm so sorry that you have to go through this. I don't even know what to say. I'm just so sorry about it."

I wiped tears from my eyes as I held him close to me. Just behind him, Erica sat at her desk, leaned back in her big, black leather chair. She removed her glasses and put the arm on the corner of her lips as she patiently waited for us to release each other. After a few moments went by, I stepped away from Blake as he handed me a Kleenex to dry my tears. He pulled the chair out for me to sit down and as I calmed myself, Erica spoke up.

"Thank you for coming on such short notice—" She smirked. "Well, maybe I should have used a different term. In any case, thank you for being here."

"Erica, I don't know what happened. I didn't do anything—"

"Ah, ah, ah. No," she smiled, "you see, I think you are under the impression that I am upset about what was just blasted across the entertainment news stations. Is that right?" I nodded my head as she stood to her feet and walked to the window overlooking the parking lot from her fourth-floor office. "No, no, no. Not at all. This is a good thing, Jae. Don't you see that?"

She smiled and looked my way, "I mean, my phone has been ringing non-stop ever since the little porno clip of you two came on the air." She laughed. "Oops, there is that word again. Anyways, I have all kind of men calling my phone, trying to get the same thing that Blake has gotten from you. Now, we all know that I don't run an escort service. You are sugar babies and that is it. Whatever you two do after that is up to you all. Some of my clients just want the time and attention. Others want to show someone off while they go out on the town and sometimes, it leads to sexual relationships. But, as you know in your contract, that is not the type of business I run. Now," she looked at the two of us, "we will definitely use this to our advantage."

Just then, her phone rang again and her smile lit up the room. I couldn't believe what I was hearing from her. I thought she would be upset, but it seemed that she was thrilled that this would increase activity in her business. As long as that happened for her, it didn't matter that everyone in the world thought I was some escort getting paid to have sex with rich men in the city. Everything I wanted to do with my life after this point seemed like it was ruined. Once they placed my face with this scandal, it was over. I was pretty sure that I would have to be a sugar baby for the rest of my life.

I looked at Blake as he sat across from me, holding my hand on the arm of his chair. "Who would do this, Blake? Did you record us?"

"Me? God no. I would never do anything like that to you. To me. Not that I am ashamed of you or anything like that, but, you know? I have an image to keep up. I don't want people to think that I am some kind of womanizer who cheats on his wife with other women. I mean, I am that guy, but I don't want people to know it. My publicist is going to have a hell of a time cleaning this mess up."

"Well, if you didn't do it, then who? Who would put a fucking camcorder in the bedroom and tape everything that we were doing?"

"I don't know, Jae. Your guess is as good as mine, but I've been thinking about it. Maybe it was one of the maids. Maybe they were upset about their pay and decided to take it out on me like this. I mean, it is highly unlikely, but I don't know."

"What about your um—that woman you live with."

"My wife?"

I glared at him. "I didn't say her title for a reason, Blake. You didn't have to throw it in my face."

"I'm sorry, Jae." He exhaled and shook his head. "You know, I've thought about her. It very well could've been her. She has her ways and I know she is upset about how things are going. I hate to think it was her, though." He rubbed his hand over his head. "She can get in a lot of trouble because I immediately got my lawyers involved with this and anything recorded without our approval is illegal. Jail time. Fines. The works. I wouldn't want to put her through that."

"If she did the crime, then she deserves the punishment —whatever it is."

"Yeah, she does. But, we have to see what the lawyers find out."

Just then, Erica ended the call. "Alright," she said, smiling, "I just set up another client with one of our women. A very PRESTIGIOUS client."

"Who?"

"James Harris."

"Wow. Big name. His account makes mine look like nothing. I didn't think he would be into something like this."

I looked at Blake with one eyebrow above the other. "Something like this? What do you mean by that?"

He smiled. "Nothing, Jae. Please don't take offense. I just thought that he was happily married, but on the outside looking in, I guess nothing ever looks like what we imagine."

"Anyways," Erica said, "back to the tape. It is clear that there was consent between the two of you. I mean, you two were into it. Nobody was forced. It was not rape or anything of that nature, so as far as I am concerned, you two are the victims. Freaky victims, but victims none the less. The person responsible though? I don't know if I should pay them or have them arrested. They are helping this business do numbers."

Just then, her phone rang again. "Hold please."

I rolled my eyes at her as she answered it, then looked at Blake. "What does this mean for us? I mean, our business is out in the open now. Everybody knows what we are doing. Everyone knows that you are sleeping around on your wife. Are you going to put me to the side now?"

He held my hand again. "Put you to the side? I would never imagine doing anything like that. Listen, like Erica said, we are the victims. I don't care how the media tries to spin it, my publicist will get behind all of this and have us looking better than we did before. And your career after this? You don't have to worry about that because I know you are. I will pay my people to erase everything from the internet. All traces of this will be gone. Who do you think was behind YouTube removing the video off their platform? You did know it was on there, didn't you?"

"Yes. I saw it briefly."

"I made it happen. That is proof that you don't have to worry about anything in the future. Ok?"

He leaned over and kissed me on the lips. I wanted to believe him, but something inside of me said that things weren't going to be as easy as he was letting on.

CHAPTER 2

Blake

"So, we are just about wrapped up, here," Erica said as she stood to her feet and walked back over to the window. "But, you guys may want to go out the back door because, there may be a little problem getting to your vehicles."

"A little problem?" I stood up and walked over to the window. Crowds of cameramen and reporters lined the sidewalk leading to the front door of the building. Security kept them at bay for the moment, but I knew it was going to be a hell of a time trying to part the crowd and get to our cars. I exhaled, then pulled my cell phone out of my pocket. "Ronald? Yes, bring the car around to the back and please be discreet. I know that you see the crowd of wolves hanging around the front door."

"Yes, sir. I will bring the car right around."

"Thank you."

I hung up the phone and then looked at Jae. She wiped tears from her eyes as she looked at her phone. "It's been doing this all freakin' morning! Random calls from random ass numbers! I don't know when to answer or when to just leave it alone! I am tired of it already and it has only been a few hours."

I rushed over to her as she seated in the chair, then kneeled in front of her just as a teardrop exploded onto her cell phone. "Hey, hey, baby, it is going to be alright. Do you believe me?" She kept looking down until I put my hands on the sides of her face and gently guided her attention towards me. "Do you believe me?"

"I don't know, Blake."

"Just trust me, ok? I have my people all over this and they will take care of it one way or the other. Things will be back to normal in no time, but for now, we just have to roll with the punches. Now, I'll make sure you get home safely and then when all of this dies down, I'll send another ride to you so you can come back to the office and get your car. I don't want you to have to worry about a thing, ok? You can trust me."

Finally, she nodded her head, then leaned forward to wrap her arms around me. "How cute," Erica said as she made her way back to her desk. "Now, you two should probably get going because I know that there will be many more people out there if you don't leave now."

I extended my hand to Jae and once she grabbed a hold of it, I got a text message from Ronald stating that he was out back waiting for us. We walked out of the office, down the back pathway to the stairs and then out the back down. Ronald waited for us, holding the door of the Maybach open until we were safely stored inside.

As soon as I got inside, I held out my hand. She took hold of it, but I shook my head. "No. I need your phone."

"My phone? Why?"

"What did I say earlier? You just have to trust me. Please?" She reluctantly handed me her phone. It buzzed a few times in my hand before I shut it off. "Now, we are done with this one." I reached beneath the front seat and pulled out a black box, then handed it to her. "Open it."

She opened the box and revealed the brand-new version of her phone. Her eyes widened as she pulled it out of the box. "New number, new phone," I said as I stretched my arm around the back of her seat. "Now, you don't have to worry about random people calling you all throughout the day. You see, I knew something like this would happen as soon as the news hit the airwaves. So, what did your man do? I made provision. I don't want you to have to deal with anything unnecessary. I already feel bad enough that these things have happened to you."

She exhaled and turned her new phone on. "Yeah, I hate it, too. But, I don't know. I am just afraid of what is going to happen later. I mean, once my name is drug all through the mud for the rest of my life."

"Baby, you are not trusting me. I told you that my people will erase anything attached to your name. It will be like you have a brand-new identity. Nobody will know about this unless they know you personally. Just trust me on this. Please."

She swiped up on her phone, uploading the different apps she used on a regular basis. "Ok. I will trust you. But, what are we doing to do now?"

"For now, we are going to get you back home and then I

am going to go to my place and get to the bottom of this. The police are there now with my publicist and my lawyers. I just had to get down here because Erica called me and said that you would be on your way. I had to see you and make sure you were alright."

"Thank you for checking on me. It means a lot."

"You mean a lot to me, Jae. You do."

We whisked past buildings as we drove down city streets. "Why can't I go back with you?"

"It is not a good idea, Jae. Now, you know I want you with me as much as possible, but I also know that there is a lot of commotion at my house and I know you don't want to deal with that. As for now, they just know your name. They don't know where you live or anything else, so you can still remain under the radar."

She huffed as she toyed around with her phone. "Alright. Trust you, right?

"Exactly."

We rolled to a stop in front of her place and after we kissed each other, I watched her until she walked into her house and after that, we drove off and headed back to my home. I couldn't believe how much my life had flipped upside down since this morning. I woke up next to Jae and then, all of a sudden, I had to watch our intimacy replayed all over the entertainment news stations and social media. I had to pull a lot of string to get the records offline, but it was worth it for us.

As soon as we drove in front of my house, cars were lined along the front. A crowd of people rushed towards our vehicle. "You don't have to be careful not to hit anyone, Ronald. If you um, accidentally bump one of them, I'm sure it will be understandable."

He chuckled. "No thank you. I don't need to be confused with what happened back in Charleston. I will do my best to stay clear of them."

People crowded the vehicle as if they were going to shove the microphone through the window just to get a statement from me. I didn't understand it much. It was just a sex tape. It didn't make sense that it became the talk of the town, but at a time where people search for news stories, I understood it. Anything to get the clicks and views up for their respective businesses.

Ronald drove me around the back of the house where none of the paparazzi could sneak past the security and then I walked inside the house. "Mr. Austin, I have some information about this recording. Please, follow me."

I followed the detective into my room. He pointed at the area just beneath the bookshelf. "Now, it was recorded from this angle which means, whoever did it, meant to do it. This was blatant. Now, that, added to the fact that the alarm didn't go off when this was done means that this all was an inside job."

"I figured as much. Now that I think about it, the door was unlocked when I came back from out of town yesterday. I didn't think much of it, you know? I figured one of the maids accidentally left it unlocked when they rushed out, but I don't know why they would purposely record anything like that."

"So, can you rule them out?"

"Yes. Yes, I would believe so."

"So, Mr. Austin, that only leaves one option. Your wife."

"My wife?" I didn't want to believe it. I knew she was upset about how things were going between us, but I never had her pegged for any of this at all. "No. No way. She wouldn't do anything like this. It would ruin us. Ruin her."

"Well, Mr. Austin, if you can rule out your help around your home, then that only leaves one other person. Someone who knows your alarm system to the point that they could disable it, come into your room and set up a camera, and then leave undetected. I mean, if not her, then who else?"

I tapped my foot on the floor and folded my arms over my chest. I didn't believe she would do something to try to sabotage my career. Just then, I reached into my pocket to check my phone. I had forgotten that I turned it off to keep it from ringing while I was in the meeting with Erica and Jae. As soon as I turned it on, my phone buzzed non-stop for the first twenty seconds.

I paged through the notifications, mostly messages from my wife, checking to see if I was ok and wondering why I wasn't answering my phone. I smiled at the thought of it. I knew she cared. There was no way she would try to check up on me like this if she was the one that did it. "Please excuse me, gentlemen. I need to take this call into another room. I will be back shortly."

"Take your time, Mr. Austin."

I left the room and went to a secluded area of the house, overlooking the front yard. The press were still camped outside, waiting for me to throw them bones so they could twist my words and make a click bait worthy story out of it. "Baby?"

"Blake?"

"Hey. I'm sorry, I've been in meetings all day long trying to figure this mess out. I don't know what is going on, but I have people here working on it now. They think—" Suddenly, I was interrupted by a maniacal laugh. I pulled the phone away from ear to make sure I knew what I was hearing, then placed it back just as her laughter simmered down. "Baby?"

"Ohh, poor thing. Your little intimate business is floating all over the internet now, huh? All over the news stations. Everywhere. That is such an adulterous shame!"

"Wait a minute, you really did this? You were behind this? The recording?" She cackled in my ear again and at that point, it clicked for me. I remembered her vow to get me back after she caught me in the shower with Jae. She wanted to get revenge, but I didn't think she would go through with. "Why? Why would you try to destroy me like this? You know what our relationship is and if you happen to destroy what I have, what do you think that means for you? You are wearing designer clothes, the latest fashion, driving the best cars that money can buy. Do you think you will still do that if my career is ruined?"

She didn't respond and it was no use trying to get one out of her. She laughed louder, mocking me. Driving me to a level of anger that I wasn't sure how to control. I didn't know what I was going to do from this point on.

CHAPTER 3

Jae

I stayed in my room for two days because I didn't want to step outside and have someone recognize me as the woman that slept with Blake Austin. Even with the new phone, people still found a way to get in touch with me. I'd been receiving phone calls from reporters who had been trying to get me to do interviews for their websites and tv shows, but I didn't want that kind of attention. I had already been through enough during the last few days and I didn't want to deal with anything else.

I tried not to be mad at Blake since he wasn't the one who recorded me, but it was difficult. I didn't understand how he could be so careless as to let something as intimate as us having sex get recorded for everyone to see. It didn't make sense and I hadn't heard from him much since he dropped me off a couple of days ago. Just like clockwork, my phone rang and his name popped up on my phone.

I rolled my eyes and answered, "What, Blake?"

"Wow. Why are you answering like that?"

I grabbed a hold of my pillow and tucked it beneath my arm. "Because of all of this shit going on. I don't know what is happening. I can't even go out the house because I am scared that somebody is going to recognize me as the hoe you slept with or something like that. I don't want to deal with it. I've been a fucking prisoner in my own got damned home, Blake, and I hate it! I fucking hate it!"

"Alright, alright, I understand, babe. Please, just calm down, ok? Look. We believe we know how the video got recorded and who did it." I perked up, waiting for him to explain more. "I think it was my wife."

"Your wife?" My eyebrows scrunched together. "You think she recorded us? But why would she do something like that?"

"I think she may have been mad about us, you know?

Payback for when she saw me in the shower with you a while back. That's what it boils down to."

"Wait. Wait a minute." I scratched my head. "Why would she be mad about us being together if you two are in an open marriage? That doesn't make any sense, Blake." He remained silent on the other line for a few moments. "Blake? I know you hear me talking to you."

"Listen, can we talk about this in person? I would feel more comfortable seeing your face while we discuss this because I know it will go over better."

"No, you can tell me now. Why the fuck is she mad if you two are in an open marriage? That shit doesn't make a lick of sense."

"Listen, I really don't know why she did it. But, she is out of pocket now. I think she has flown to Belize and she is not answering any of my calls. I don't know what to think about her right now, but it is hard to come to conclusions without speaking to her. Right now, it is just guesses, you know? We have an open marriage, but I may have disrespected the terms of our agreement. That's all."

"That's all?"

"That's it. Now, like I said, I want to talk to you about it more in person because I think it will be better for us. Can you afford me that time with you? Please?"

I thought about Darryl. I knew he had probably already heard the news about me and I was sure it made things much worse between us than it already was. Sadly, I missed him. I missed him more than I could even admit to his face because I knew he wouldn't take my calls. "Jae?"

"You know what, Blake? I need to go, ok? I'll have to talk to you another time."

"Jae, please, just—"

I hung up the phone and tossed it to the side. He called me back seconds later, but I ignored the call and laid on my side. I just wanted all of this shit to be over and it seemed like it never would. I wanted my life back. I wanted to be able to go outside without the fear of having cameras shoved in my face, begging me for answers to questions that I had no idea how to respond to. I wished Darryl would show up out of nowhere like he always seemed to do whenever I needed him. He was a light at a dark time for me and right now, it was exactly what I needed.

I just wanted all of this madness to go away and right

now, it seemed as if it wasn't going to happen any time soon. Just then, there was a knock at my door. "Go away."

She door opened immediately and Angie stood on the other side. "Umm, somebody is out here at the door for you and I don't know who she is. You said you didn't want no company, but she is still out there. I'm bout ready to fade this bitch, but I figured I would come and let you know what was going on before shit started poppin'."

I snatched the covers off my body and climbed out of bed. If it was another news reporter coming over here to beg for a story, I didn't know what I was going to do. Angie had already told three of them to fuck off in the last few hours and right now, I was liable to go crazy just to teach them a lesson. I walked to the door and before I could say anything, my eyes lit up. Shayla stood on the other side with her hands propped on her hips and her head tilted to the side. "Um, are you going to let me in now?"

I was at ease as soon as I saw Shayla standing on the other side of the door. I unlocked the latch and pushed it open for her to come in. "Girl, there has been so many random reporters coming over here the last few days that I told my sister not to let anybody else in."

"Yeah," she said as she stepped inside, "it seemed like she wanted to snatch the door open and put hands on me. I ain't come here for all that, though. I just wanted to check on my best friend."

I looked at Angie as she stood off to the side, waiting for an explanation. "Angie, this is my best friend, Shayla. Shayla, this is my sister Angie."

"I'm sorry about that earlier, girl. I was just looking out for my sister."

"No, boo, it's cool. I get it. You gotta watch out for her, especially with all the bullshit floating around now." We all sat down on the couch as she continued, "I almost had to touch a couple broads up for disrespecting you. They are calling you all types of names. Homewrecker, prostitute. Everything. But, I didn't let it last long."

"This shit is going to fucking ruin my life and everything I wanted to do further down the line. My name is shit. I don't even know what the fuck I'm going to do with my life after this."

"Jae, people will forget about this," Shayla said. "Nobody has a long-term memory these days. They hear stuff, it is poppin' for a few days and then after that, they are waiting for the new wave or next person to talk shit about. It happens."

"I just don't want it to stick with me." I exhaled and shook my head. Angie turned on the television and as soon as it came on, my name had just left the news reporter's lips. "Please turn it off," I said as I grabbed a pillow and held it close.

She turned the television off and put the remote on the table. "It is going to blow over, Jae. I know it is."

"I'm thinking about quitting the sugar baby shit. I can't have my life getting ruined based on some bullshit like this. If a petty ass woman is going to do this to try to expose her husband, then there ain't no tellin' what else another one might try to do later. I don't even want to put myself through this shit again."

"Quitting?" Shayla asked. "Damn. I mean, I hear you and everything, but you are willing to walk away from all of that money?"

"Shit, I would rather have my piece than that money. Besides that, I don't know what the fuck I am going to do if something like this, or worse, happens. I need to focus on getting my shit together and preparing for the future because I'm not going to have this body, or my looks, for the rest of my life. I need to move on."

"Yeah, I been tellin' you that, Jae," Angie said as she folded her legs beneath her, "might as well focus on yo' shit and get it together. I mean, I hate that it has happened, but maybe something like this needed to happen to get you on the right track. Something to push you out and make you see things differently. It took some bullshit for me to leave the strip club, but after it happened, I was able to get the fuck up out of there."

"Yeah. Yeah," Shayla said, "she is right. Maybe it is time for you to get up out of the business. You said his wife was behind it all?"

"Yeah. I mean, that is what he thinks. He said the bitch skipped town to Belize or some shit like that. He said it was an open marriage, but the more this shit comes out in the open, the less I believe it was an open marriage. That mutha fucka was probably just cheating on his wife like every other dude."

"Damn. Well, yeah, I can't blame you if you want to leave. I mean, the other option would be to just beat her ass one good time and she will learn her lesson after that."

"I ain't tryin' to catch a case over a bitch, so I don't want do that. I think I'ma just call Erica and let her know that I am out. That is the best thing for me to do."

Shayla exhaled as she sat on the couch across from me. I knew that I was probably disappointing her because I wanted to step out of the business, but I hoped she understood. I had already lost a friend in Darryl and I would hate to lose another one because of my choices. Shayla stood up and wrapped her purse around her shoulder. "Well, I'm about to go. Let me know if you need anything, Jae. I'll be here for you whenever you call."

"Thank you, Shayla. But—" I stood up. "I just don't want you to be mad at me for leaving the business. You are a good friend and I wouldn't want anything to come between us like that."

"Mad at you? Baby, no, I wouldn't be mad at you for doing what's best for you. Personally, I think you are right about this shit. We can't do this forever and if you can find a way out right now, then take it. I won't be mad at you for that. Go to school. Start a business. Do what you have to do, boo, I am still going to be here either way. Ok?"

"Thank you, Shayla."

I wrapped my arms around her and then watched her walk out of the house. I figured I would go to Erica's office tomorrow and let her know what I wanted to do. I had to tell her face-to-face just so she could see that I was serious about it all.

CHAPTER 4

"Erica, I need to—"

I stopped after I burst open her door without knocking. I had already fought my way through a sea of paparazzi and news reporters, so I didn't feel like waiting for her to open the door for me. She was seated in front of her desk with three men scattered in chairs on the other side. "And this is one of my best workers. Jae? I'd like you to meet Aaron, David and Hank."

I could feel their eyes crawling over me, undressing me with their eyes. I shrugged the thought away. "I need to speak with you, Erica. This cannot wait."

She smiled. "Alright, I understand. Gentlemen? Do you mind giving us a moment?"

"I like the fire in her," one of the men said. "Is she available?"

Erica stood to her feet, haughty. "Well, I shall let you know one way or the other. But, if she is not, I am sure that after you browse our catalogue, you will find someone to suit your needs. Alright?" With that, she extended her arm to lead me out of the room.

I scoffed at the men, then made my way out and into the lobby. "This couldn't have waited, Jae? I was just in the middle of closing the deal on a few wealthy clients. Ever since this little scandal between you and Blake kicked off, things have skyrocketed for me."

"Well, I am glad that your business is taking off to new heights because my life is hitting new lows at the same time. That is the reason I came down here."

"Now, I know that your life is flipped upside down right now, but that is temporary. Before you know it, things will—"

"I want out, Erica."

She stopped mid-sentence. Her eyebrows furrowed. "I'm sorry?"

"I want out. I am tired of getting harassed by reporters. I

am tired of going out in public just to see people glaring at me like that haven't seen a cheater before. Hell, half of the women that look at me that way are probably getting cheated on by their husbands, too. I am just tired of it. I don't want to do this anymore."

She waited a few moments and looked to the side. I was ready to combat her about anything she wanted to bring up and no matter what she said, I wasn't going to give in. I had my mind set up. Finally, she spoke. "Alright."

I tilted my head to the side. "Alright?"

"Follow me, please."

Without another word, she turned and began walking out of the lobby, leading me down a short corridor and into another office. She opened the door and went to a filing cabinet in the corner of the room. I watched her as she paged through the manila folders until she found what she was looking for. She licked her finger and pulled out a small stack of papers, then handed them to me and pushed the drawer closed again.

I took it from her hand. "What is this?"

"Your contract." She exhaled and leaned against the desk. "You know that this is an at-will relationship. Whenever either of us wants to terminate it, the contract has to be terminated as well. I understand that we had a 2-year deal, but with the way things are picking up for me right now, I don't think I will have a problem gathering more girls or pulling in more clients. So, if you want to leave, then please. By all means, I do not want to hold you here against your will."

I hated the way she was going about the issue. I wanted more of a fight. More of a desire to keep me here, but now, I really knew where we stood. "So, do I just rip this up or what? You want me to do that?"

She laughed. "Rip it up? No. Please read section three."

I turned to the page and read through it. My mouth slowly opened as I read it from the first word to the last word in the section. "Give you the money back? Wait, is this real?" She didn't say a word. I continued, "It says that I need to return all money given to me by the client and discontinue any services that the client is providing for me. How am I supposed to do this, Erica?"

"That is not up to me, Jae. That is totally up to you and this has always been in the contract. I trust that you have kept your copy of this as well, right? Right. It has not been altered in any way. All of those things need to be returned, and or discontinued. You will not be able to benefit from sugar baby if you are not a part of the program anymore. You can't continue to profit off the fruits without being a part of the tree, Jae."

I couldn't believe what I was hearing. Not only did I not have the money to give back, but if I had to discontinue everything with Blake, then my aunt would be snatched out of rehab, my school would be cancelled and in no time, I would be back in the projects living the same life as before. I couldn't take that risk. She had me cornered and she knew it. "I can't pay this back, Erica. You want me to pay back money from months ago?"

"Yes. Every cent is accounted for and," she smiled, "I know that Blake is providing for you and your family right now. All of that will come to an end. You see, I make sure my ass and my assets are covered when doing business like this. If my women were just able to walk out of their contract at any moment, then my business would fail. You entered an agreement with me and both parties fully expected the agreement to be completed."

"And, what if I don't? What if I just say 'fuck you' and walk away from all this shit?"

She shrugged. "It won't go away. I will pursue you legally if I have to. Sugar baby is not a game, Jae. This is a business. A well-structured one at that, so, we take the necessary precautions while running this program. I hope that you understand that. This is not personal, Jae. This is business. Now, if you want to walk away, like I said, please, go. But, we would also love to have you stay and finish out the term. The choice is yours."

I dropped the contract on the table in front of us. My heartbeat picked up its pace. Beads of sweat formed on my brow and suddenly, the room spun on an axis. I put my hand on the desk to keep balance as all the thoughts of what my life would plummet into surfaced in my mind. "Jae?" Erica asked, her voice becoming fainter by the moment. "Jae, are you ok?"

Suddenly, I tipped over and fell onto the floor. The last thing I heard was Erica's voice as she rushed to my side and stood over me. "Jae! Jae, what is going on! Jae!"

Blake

"She is what?"

"She is in the hospital. She came here to talk to me about her contract and, before I knew it, she passed out. I called an ambulance for her and she is at the hospital now."

"Which one?"

"St. Michaels."

"Alright. I am headed up there now."

I had called Jae's phone earlier to check on her and, when she didn't respond, I figured that I would give Erica a call to find out if she knew anything. I never expected to hear her tell me that Jae passed out and had to be rushed to the hospital. She went up there to talk about her contract and, and that moment, I was afraid of why.

I went to the hospital as soon as I could. As soon as I got there, I squinted my eyes at a familiar face. *No way*, I said to myself as I got closer. Shayla sat in the waiting area with her phone in her hand, oblivious to the fact that I had just stepped into the room. I shook my head, wondering how she knew I was here. A part of me wanted to believe that she was the one who set up the camera in my home, but I knew that was highly unlikely.

I thought back to the days when I used to be a client of hers. She got into a huge confrontation with my wife at that time and it resulted in the police being called to my place and me having to discontinue my relationship with her. But, if that didn't happen, I never would've met Jae, so I took that as a blessing. After standing near the entry for a few moments, I finally decided to approach her and figure out what the hell was going on.

"Shayla."

She immediately lifted her attention towards me. "Blake?"

"What the hell are you doing here?"

"Um," she smiled, "well, hello to you, too."

"I am not here for the pleasantries. Why are you following me and how did you know I would be here?"

She laughed. "Well, that is very arrogant of you. Just to think that I am wasting my time to follow you around this fucking city. That is highly arrogant."

"Just cut the shit, ok?" I sat down beside her, trying to keep my voice down and the attention off of me. "What are you doing here?"

"My friend was rushed to the hospital and I came here to check on here. Why is that important to you?"

"Because I am here, too!"

"Oh, shit. Well, excuse me, your highness. I didn't know

that I couldn't be in the same place as 'royalty.' Fucking bastard. Get over yourself. I am here for my friend, Jae. She was rushed in almost an hour ago. I don't have time to waste, stalking you. Get over yourself."

"Wait a minute. Your friend Jae?"

"Yes. I didn't stutter."

"Bullshit."

She rolled her eyes. "Look, I have better things to do than to argue with you about who I am here to see. You are not on my list, and I never planned for you to be on my list of people to see. So, if you want to continued rambling on about how I am here just for you, then go right ahead. I am going to continued waiting for MY FRIEND so I can go in and check on her after they finish running tests. Ok?"

She switched her attention back to her phone as I sat down beside her. It seemed as if she was telling the truth, and the more I thought about it, the more her response had become plausible. She did work in the same organization as Jae, so her story wasn't far-fetched. Finally, I got up and walked over to the desk to ask about Jae.

They told me which room she was in and, in that

moment, we had been cleared to go into the room and check on her. I looked at Shayla as she stood to her feet. I missed her a little bit. The way she pleased me in the bedroom. Her ass was still as fat as I remembered, but she had nothing on Jae. Shayla only had me physically, but Jae had me mentally and emotionally as well. It was no contest.

I followed Shayla to the room with the nurse. Once the door opened, I saw Jae laying in bed with another woman standing beside her. She was fast asleep. "Who is he?" the woman asked.

"I am Blake."

"Oh—" She smiled. "So, you're Blake? I see."

I walked over to Jae as she slept peacefully on her bed. Even though I knew she would be ok, I hated to see her in this position. I was helpless.

CHAPTER 5

Jae

I slowly opened my eyes to see that I was in a hospital room. I looked down at my arms. Tubes were connected to me with small things poked into my veins. My eyebrows scrunched together. *What happened?* The last thing I remembered was me lying on the floor, in Erica's office, while she rushed to my side. Next thing I knew, I was in here.

That was when I heard their voices just ahead of the bed I'd been lying on. It was Blake and Shayla, going back and forth with each other. I closed my eyes so I could eavesdrop on the conversation because from what I heard, it seemed as if it was intense.

"You are not friends with her, Shayla, and if you are, it sure as hell is not genuine."

"What are you talking about? You don't know me or who I am friends with. We are in the same business, Blake. Stop acting like it is some im-fucking-possible thing to conceive that I am friends with her."

"Bullshit," he replied in a hushed tone. "Fucking bull-shit. I know you and I know how twisted and maniacal you can be. You are the fucking reason my ex-wife attacked you when she did. You have a fucking bad atti-tude and you do what you want to get what you want. Vindictive little—"

"You better watch your mouth, Blake. You know you don't want to bring the old me out in this little room. You know how I can get. You know how I am when you call me out of my name."

I heard footsteps in the room. "Get away from me, Shayla. Are you serious? Are you going to try to do something sexual in here? I am done with you. I've been done with you since our BUSINESS relationship ended a long time ago."

"Oh, cut the shit, Blake! What is wrong with you? Getting yourself in this situation with that little girl?

You let yourself get fucking recorded while you two were having sex and then allowed it to get played everywhere in the fucking world? Seriously? The Blake I knew would never allow anything like this to happen!"

"Well, sometimes, shit happens that is out of my control and that is exactly what went down this time."

"Umhmm, all I am saying is that you are slipping. You are letting your feelings get involved in this shit and that is why it is dangerous. You can't even see a threat coming before it happens and in that state of mind, I'm surprised nothing else has happened to this point."

"Isn't that what happened to you, with me?"

"Yes, and you see how that turned out." She exhaled, then continued, "And then, to top it off, you rushed up here to see her once you found out she was in the hospital? Huh? I can't believe that you are even giving her this much attention! I never got anything like this from you! Why!?"

"I knew it. I knew you were just befriending her to keep an eye on me and what we were doing so you could compare. I could see right through your tired little charade."

I couldn't believe what I was hearing. I had no idea that

Blake and Shayla were involved before me and to find out that Shayla was only my friend because of Blake had started making sense. She was always curious about what we had going on and what we were doing. I never told her much because I was unsure why she was so inquisitive, but now, it all made sense.

Shayla continued, "Oh, stop! You are acting real brand new, Blake. You think I was just going to let you walk away from me like that? Request another girl? After all we had been through? After all we have done with each other? Just to watch you treat this little girl better than you've ever treated me? Huh? What does she have that I don't? I know it is not ass or titties. I know she can't suck your dick like I do, and I know for a fact that she can't do the tricks I can do in the bedroom. So, what the fuck is it about her that you couldn't have with me?"

Just then, I opened my eyes and made it known that I was no longer asleep. They both shot their attention in my direction. "Jae? My goodness, Jae. Are you alright?" Blake asked as he rushed to my bed. "I came down here as soon as I heard."

He tried to reach for me, but I put a hand up. "Stop. Don't touch me."

He looked at me with a confused expression, "What? Why not? What did I do?"

"She heard the conversation," Shayla said as she folded her arms over her chest. "That is the only reason she would be acting like this now. Am I right?"

"I heard enough."

"Jae, it is not what you think. Trust me, it is not what you think."

"So, you didn't have a relationship with Shayla before me? Huh?" I looked at Shayla. "And you didn't befriend me just so you could keep tabs on what I was doing with Blake? Because that is what I heard, so please inform me if I am wrong. I would love nothing more than to be wrong about that right now."

Neither one of them responded as I looked back and forth at their blank expressions. I continued, "Yeah, that's what I thought."

Shayla sucked her teeth. "Look, I only came down here to make sure that you were alright, and now that I see you are," she grabbed her purse off the chair, "I don't see any reason to remain." She glared at Blake, then rolled her eyes and in moments, she left the room.

"Jae, I'm sorry. I didn't—"

"You could've at least told me, Blake. At least have the common decency to tell me that you had something going on with my friend. Well, the bitch who pretended to be my friend."

"I didn't know you two were even communicating with each other until I saw her in the lobby. I didn't know about it. Please, Jae, you have to believe that if I knew about it, I would tell you."

"Oh, so you're saying you wouldn't lie to me, huh? The same way you didn't lie about you and your wife being in an open marriage? Right?" He looked away from me. I shook my head. "Yeah, I knew it. I knew it was all a fucking lie. You are trying to play two sides of the fence. You want to make me believe that you wouldn't lie to me, but at the same time, you lied to me about something else. Something much more serious. You are a joke, Blake. A complete joke."

"Listen, Jae, you are in the hospital recovering from whatever episode you had to get you in here. I just want to make sure that you are ok before we start talking about anything else."

"Start talking about it? No, boo, we are done talking about it. We are done with all of this shit. I went to Erica to talk to her about my contract and what I needed to do to get out of it. She said I had to return all of the money and discontinue any services that you are providing for me, and if that is the case, then I will do it. I will pull my aunt out of rehab and make sure she stays clean. I will find a way to get a loan and pay my own way through college. I will do what I have to do because I refuse to put up with you and anymore bullshit at the agency. This whole ordeal has stripped away my privacy and put me in a hospital. I don't want anything else to do with it."

"I know you are upset, Jae, and you have every right to be. But, you don't need to go making rash decisions like this based off emotion. I think you should really gather yourself and think about what you are doing and what it means for you down the line. You know where you were before all of this and—"

"How dare you? How fucking dare you say that to me? You think I need you to survive? You think I need this agency? No. Fuck you and fuck sugar baby. Fuck all of that shit. I'll be fine and I will figure out a way to get through it all."

"That is not what I mean, Jae. You are jumping to conclusions."

"And you can jump in the middle of fucking traffic, Blake. I trusted you. I trusted you when you told me that shit about your wife. I trusted you when you said how much you cared about me and how much things were different between us and, you know what?" I wiped a stream of tears from my eyes, "I believed you. I honestly believed you. I thought things would work out differently for us. I thought that somehow, we would end up together later down the line without the contracts. Without the money exchanges. I don't know why, but I thought that for a moment. Now, I see that is a pure fairytale. That shit doesn't come true for real. Not for women like me."

"Jae—"

"Just get out."

"Jae, if you just let me—"

"Get the fuck out!"

Just then, the doctor walked into the room. I covered my face to hide the tears as he spoke up. "Is everything alright in here?"

"Yes, doctor," I said, speaking from behind the palm of my hand. "He was just leaving."

I removed my hand from over my face and just as Blake turned away and walked out of the room with his head hanging and his shoulders slumped to the side. "Do you need me to call security to stay nearby?"

"No. He is not a dangerous man. We just had a disagreement. That's all."

"I see." He pulled out his notepad. "Well, I am happy to see that you are awake. Let me ask you, do you have issues with panic attacks or anxiety?" I nodded my head. "I see. And is there something that caused you to pass out before you were brought here?" I nodded my head again. "Ok. Well, that seems to be the case. You passed out because of an anxiety attack. Are you on any medications at all?"

"No. I haven't been on any meds for any issues that I have."

"Ok. I am going to prescribe something for you, but honestly, I think the best thing for you would be therapy. Have someone who you can talk to. Someone who can help you come back down to earth whenever you start having one of those anxiety attacks. Those things can be overwhelming, as I am sure you already know. I have a few that I know personally. A few therapists that can help aid you in this process. I will get their information for you if you want."

"Yes, please. Thank you, doctor."

"No problem. I will send the nurse in with that information, but after that, you are all set. You should be able to go home in a bit, so just sit tight for a moment. Ok?"

"Ok. Thank you."

He smiled and left the room. I thought about Blake and how much he had been helping me. I was sure that he would pay for any therapy that I needed, but since I was going to leave the company, I knew that wasn't an option. I would have to figure all of this out on my own. I just hoped that I would be able to get through it. The last thing I wanted was to end up worse off than what I started.

CHAPTER 6

"Take it easy, Jae. You just fell out yesterday and you're trying to do everything on your own."

"I'm not crippled, Angie. I can walk on my own." She helped me over to the couch and sat down beside me. The hospital let me go home that same day and I was glad to be out of there. I didn't want to stay in that place any longer than I had to.

Angie grabbed the remote, but I was afraid of what would come on when she pressed power. Maybe someone would have information about me being in the hospital, or even worse, I could still be the poster child for whores around the world. Either way, I wanted no part of it. "Wait, Angie. Don't turn on the TV."

"Don't worry, Jae, I haven't been watching the entertainment news for a couple of days now. It is not the last channel on." I waited cautiously as the television flickered on and once I saw a different channel, I was relieved. I still knew that my name was floating around and being dragged through the mud and as soon as I realized it, I started crying. "Jae, what's wrong?"

"Everything is wrong, Angie. Everything." I wiped the stream of tears from my eyes. "I don't want to be a sugar baby anymore. I went to Erica to talk to her about it, but when she told me what I had to do to get out, I knew it was almost impossible."

"What do you have to do?"

"I have to return all the money that was given to me. And, in addition to that, I have to discontinue any benefits I receive from being a sugar baby. Money, payments, everything. And that means I would have to take auntie out of rehab and I can kiss my fucking college tuition goodbye. I am fucking trapped. I want to get out, but I can't. I just can't."

"You can, Jae."

"How?"

She exhaled. "Just do it. If you have to give the money

back, just give it back and I'll—I'll take up stripping again if I have to."

"What? No. I couldn't let you do that."

She twisted her face. "Let me? You don't have to 'let me' do anything, Jae. I'll do it if I please. But, at the same time, you've held us down for so long. You worked and paid for everything. The least I could do is return the favor until you figured things out on your own."

I swiped another row of tears from my cheeks. "I would feel horrible if you went back to stripping just so I didn't have to be a sugar baby again. How is that fair to you? You stepped away so you could go to school and get your life on the right track. What do I look like putting you back in a position you hated in the first place?"

"You would look like a sister who needs her sister. You wouldn't look any less strong to me. We all need help and when I needed help, you were right there, bussin' your ass just to give it to me. You deserve this, Jae. You deserve a break."

I appreciated the fact that she wanted to do that for me. It showed me how much she truly loved me and had my back, but I couldn't allow her to sacrifice her life for me. I had to figure out another way to make things work. "Look, I can't do that. I'll just—I'll still be a sugar baby, but I won't work with Blake anymore. I'll just let Erica know that I need another client. I'm sure she won't have a problem finding one for me with all the attention her business is getting these days. And, with me being the face of it, I know that a lot of men will probably want me."

"Want to have sex with you. If they are seeing you based off that recording, then I am sure that is what they will want from you. Things are going to change for you, sis. They are going to want more and I know it is not an escort service, but how are you going to tell men 'no' when they saw you fucking another client? They will believe that they are going to get the very same thing."

"Then they will be in for a rude awakening."

"But that will decrease the number of guys that want you."

"Well, maybe you are on to something. If Erica has to terminate the contract, then I won't have to give any of the money back. That is in the fine print. In the same section she made me read when I was trying to get out of it yesterday. It could work."

"It could. But, I don't mind getting back on that pole if I

have to. I mean, I don't want to, but I would do it for you in a heartbeat."

"Thank you, but I want to figure out another way before that has to happen."

"Ok," she leaned back on the couch. "So, I met Blake earlier today. He is not what I expected, but he is still cute."

I rolled my eyes at the mention of his name. I hated that he was even there to begin with and after I found out he had history with Shayla, it made things even worse. "Fuck him. I am done. He is a fucking liar. He told me that he was in an open marriage with his wife, but it is clear that he was lying about that. And, on top of it all, he was in a relationship with Shayla before me."

"Shayla? The girl that came to visit you yesterday and at the hospital?"

"Yes. He was her client before he came to me. I don't know what happened between them that made it end, but I overheard them when they thought I was asleep in the hospital room. They were arguing back and forth about it and it turns out that Shayla was only my friend because she wanted to keep tabs on Blake. She was a fake ass friend."

"Wow, really? Damn. See, I knew I didn't like that broad when I met her in the beginning. It was something about her, but you said she was your friend, so I just left it alone. But, I knew something was up. I knew it."

"It is what it is. But, both of them can fucking play in traffic for all I care. I don't want to see either of them again from this point on. I just want my life to go back to normal. I want to be able to walk out in public without people gawking at me. I want to go to college and let all of this shit fall behind me. That's all I want."

"You deserve it, Jae. But honestly, I thought it was something else going on between you and Blake. I mean, you didn't talk about him much in the beginning, but I remember you mentioning him from time to time."

I thought back to the early days between us. The times he made me feel like I was the only woman in the world, even though I knew that I wasn't. He painted a perfect picture of who he was, or at least, who I thought he was. Now, I know it was all just an act and, if he was serious about me, he would've left his wife a long time ago, but he was still married to her and it didn't look like he planned on going anywhere.

"Yeah, I thought I loved him at one point. I had never

met anyone like him before. The way he pampered me. The way he bought me whatever I wanted and treated me like a queen whenever I was around him. I wasn't used to that. I guess that is what I was drawn to. It wasn't love though." I exhaled and thought about Darryl. The way he made me feel had nothing to do with gifts or what he could buy me. It was about his touch. His conversation. Our chemistry. Everything that money couldn't buy, and I knew that was love. It had to be.

"But Darryl? The way I feel about Darryl is not the same. I think love is Darryl. No, you know what? I know for a fact that love is Darryl."

"Then fix it."

"Fix it? He is not returning my calls and by now, I know he has seen the video of me all over the fucking place. He doesn't want anything to do with me and I know it. Besides that, I am damaged goods and no man wants damaged goods."

"Oh, please, Jae. Damaged goods? Seriously? Look, any man that thinks he is getting a woman who has not fucked another man is a fucking idiot. There ain't no such things as twenty-year-old virgins anymore. That shit only happens in movies and fairytales. Or bitches that still let their lives be controlled by their parents. That's it. You are not damaged goods."

"I feel like it."

"But you aren't, so stop saying that. Darryl is not like that though. I still talk to him and, believe it or not, he still cares about you. We haven't talked about the recording or anything because we haven't spoken in a few days, but I know he cares. I think you should just call him. I bet you would be surprised of his reaction."

"Surprised at how he cusses me out and makes me feel like shit?"

She laughed. "No, Jae, not at all. See, your problem is that you overthink too much. You let your mind take you to places you have no business going. You just need to put that shit to the side and live. Pick up your phone, call him and see how much you are wrong about the way he thinks of you. That what needs to happen. He cares about you, Jae, and it is not just physical, either."

I wanted to call him with everything in me, but I was afraid of the rejection. Afraid of the words that he would send straight for my heart. As much as I loved and cared for him, I wasn't sure if I could take that sort of abuse at a time like this. "I don't know, Angie. I think

I just need some more time to convince myself that he doesn't hate me. Maybe give him some more time, too, especially if he has saw the recording. I just think we both need time."

She shrugged her shoulders. "Alright. But, like I said, it is not as bad as you think. He still loves you and that won't go away over bullshit. If you talk to him, he will answer, and he won't be a dick about it. Don't let yourself be tricked into missing out on a good man because of your fears."

She grabbed the remote and flipped through the channels. I got up to leave before she danced across one of the entertainment news stations. In my room, I laid in the bed and tucked myself underneath the covers. I thought about Darryl and what I would give to feel his arms draped around my body right now. I felt so at peace whenever I was with him and I hated the fact that I traded him away for the bullshit I was going through now. I grabbed my phone and scrolled through the contacts until I landed on his name. I couldn't bring myself to dial out. I put the phone down, turned over on the other side and tried to force myself to go to sleep.

CHAPTER 7

"Are you serious? This is the fourth time this week. What the fuck am I going to do with all of these flowers? Start a garden?"

"Shit, I don't know, but if you don't want this bracelet, I'll take it off your hands."

I took it away from Angie. "No. I'm sending this shit back just like I sent all the other shit back. He does not get the point, that persistent little fucker."

"You're really sending this back? This bracelet has to be worth at least ten bands. You're just going to give it back?"

I threw it into the box. "Yes. All of it. He is going to understand, one way or the other, that I don't want anything to do with him anymore. I am done with it. Finished."

She shrugged her shoulders and left the room as I packed the things back up and prepared to return them right to his house. He had done everything he could to pull me back into his web of deceit, but I had no desire to. Just then, my phone rang. I saw his name flash across the screen. My call log was filled with missed and ignored calls from him.

"Angie, can you please come in here? Now."

She quickly rushed into the room. "Are you about to give me the bracelet?"

"No, but can you answer this and put it on speaker? It is Blake. Tell him that I don't want to talk to him anymore. Whenever I say it, he doesn't get the picture."

She took the phone out of my hand and put it on speaker. "Hello?"

"Ja—wait, hello? Is this Jae?"

"No, this is her sister."

"Oh, the one that was at the hospital with her last week?"

"Yes. How are you doing?"

"I'm fine. Look, she told me to answer the phone because she didn't want to talk to you. She told me to tell you to stop calling her because she doesn't want anything to do with you anymore."

I nodded my head as I put the things back into the box. "I understand that is what she said, but I need her to know that I care about her. My life has been a mess ever since I haven't been able to talk to her. I need her in my life and, I know she is listening. I hope she is. She needs to hear this. She needs to know that for the past months we have been involved, I have been on cloud nine and she is the reason for it. Please, I just—I just want to see her. Talk to her. I miss her so much."

Angie looked at me. She didn't know what to say and, I don't know how he did it, but he was able to make me feel sorry for him. I heard the pain in his voice, and I could imagine what he looked like. His sad, droopy eyes. His long mouth. His bottom lip poked out. I exhaled, then took the phone from Angie. "What do you want from me, Blake?"

"I just want to see you. I just want to talk to you in person. That's all I need. I know you hate me, and you have every reason to. I have damn near ruined your life in more ways than one and I am sorry, but there is no amount of gifts or phone conversations I can have with you that can convey that more than a face to face conversation. So, if you are willing, please—just let me talk to you."

I looked at Angie. She nodded her head as if I should give him that chance he desired. I looked at the flowers on the bed and the bracelet shinning inside of the box like glitter when the sun hit the diamonds. "Alright. You can come, but that doesn't mean that we are working anything out and it doesn't mean that I will still let you be my client. This is just a talk, so please don't come over here with expectations that won't be fulfilled. You will leave here disappointed if you do."

"Ok, I got it. Your rules, your way. You just tell me when you want me to come over and I will be there."

"I'll text you when I am ready. It should be later today though. Oh, and Blake? Please don't send any more gifts because you are just wasting money. I have sent them all back to you for a reason."

"Ok. I won't send anything else."

"You can send me some jewelry though, Blake!" Angie shouted out.

I hissed at her to shut her mouth, then spoke into the phone, "No, don't send her anything. I don't want anything else from you, ok?"

"Alright. Just text me when you are ready for me to come and I will be on my way."

"Ok."

I hung up the phone and looked at Angie. She shrugged her shoulders. "What? Don't blame me for trying. That man has money to lose and if he wants to send me a diamond bracelet just because I am your sister, then I don't think you should be a hater. Just let it happen!"

I shook my head, then shooed her out of my room so I could get ready for him to show up. I didn't plan on wearing anything fancy. Just something to get out of the clothes I had been lounging around the house in for the past few days. Things had finally started dying down about the sex tape and I was sure that I could go out of the house if I needed to, but I just didn't feel like it. I grabbed a jogging suit, then sent the text to Blake to let him know he could come.

As soon as I opened the door, I could tell that he was

different. He didn't have the same energetic look that I was used to seeing on him. Bags were beneath his eyes. His white tee shirt looked worn and out of shape. His jogging pants fit tight around his legs as if they were too small for him. Stubble formed along the edges of his face. "Hey, Jae."

"Blake? Um—come in."

He stepped inside and I led him to the back of the house and onto the patio. Two lawn chairs were positioned towards the declining sun as it sent the orangish rays across the atmosphere. "So, here we are," he said as we sat down on the chairs. "This is a beautiful view of the sunset. Peaceful. I haven't had a lot of that these last few days."

"I can understand why. How is everything back home?"

"Just as stressful as it has ever been. The police back to me about the recording. They have officially ruled my wife out as a suspect."

My eyebrows lifted on my forehead. "What? Ruled out? I thought you knew it was her."

"No, everyone had a strong feeling that it was her. In the beginning, I didn't think she was good for it, but when I talked to her that day? The way she acted over the phone? I kind of felt like she did it after that. But, it turns out that she didn't."

"Wow. So, then who?"

He shrugged his shoulders, "I have no idea. That is just another thing I am stressing over. I have no idea who got into my house. I have no idea how they got in and why the alarm didn't go off. I mean, I've got so many questions and I don't even know how I will get the answers. It is all crazy to me."

I was sure she was good for it. It made no sense for it to be anyone else, but now, I was more afraid. Somebody snuck into his home and had us recorded. Who knows if they recorded it and watched us at the same time? "Anyways, I know that you spoke to Erica and ended the contract between us. I called her because you weren't talking to me and she told me that you ended it. I was crushed when I heard it."

He smiled, but I could tell it was just to hide the pain. "I hoped it was all a dream because of what you meant to me, but, I guess it is not. I guess it is all going to end sooner than I wanted it to."

I squinted and folded my arms over my chest. "Yeah, it was time, Blake. It was time. I mean, I know you weren't going to leave your wife for me or anything like that. So, for me, it was just false hope. Something that I wanted to happen, but I knew it wouldn't. I knew you would stay with her and you are, right?"

He shoved his hands into his pockets. "Yeah. I mean, she is not behind the recording and that would've been a reason for me to divorce her right away. So, I don't have a reason to do it right now. And I know she won't go away easily. There has to be a good reason for it to happen, you know?"

I don't know why, but I would've been at ease if he said he would choose me over her. Maybe because I hated the idea of him choosing someone over me, especially after as much as we had done together. All the things he had said to me. All the things that we said to each other. I wanted him to put me first, but right now, I knew it would never happen. I guess it was something that I need to hear to bring the closure that I needed.

"Yeah. Maybe it is best for you to just work on your marriage and let this dissolve. I think that is what will work best for both of us. Besides, after hearing about you and Shayla, I don't think we could go back to how things were before. I had to end it. I had to end the relationship between us."

He sighed. "Yeah, I get it. Trust me, I do. It doesn't make it any easier though. And listen, I know that you are supposed to give everything back, but you don't have to. I'm not going to force you to do it and there is nothing that Erica can do to make me take my money back from you. Most men would want to, especially if things ended sourly between them the way they are between us, but you mean more to me than that. Just keep it."

"No, I don't—"

"Just keep it. I won't take it back even if you tried to give it to me. I sort of feel like I owe you for all the things I have put you through in the last week. So, just keep it."

I felt good hearing him say that and a part of me wanted to reach over and give him a hug. Tell him that maybe we can work though this because I knew that deep down inside, he cared for me deeply. But, it was too late for all of that. We had too much to get over and beside all of that, he had a wife that he would never leave and I couldn't stop thinking about Darryl. We both had new paths of life to take. I just hoped mine would end on a good note.

He stood up. "Well, I won't take any more of your time. Thank you for talking to me and like I said, I just wanted to see you one more time before it was all said and done. If you need me for anything, Jae, anything—I'll be there. Ok?"

I nodded my head as I watched him walked off the patio. I remained silent until I heard the front door close behind him. It was over and now, I had to focus on rebuilding my life from here on out.

CHAPTER 8

Blake

I drove home with the music off because I didn't feel like listening to anything. I didn't think any music could change my mood, so I wanted to keep it quiet. As I rolled to a red light, I couldn't help but think about Jae. She was perfect for me and I slowly started wishing that Carissa set up the recording in my room. I wanted her to be the culprit so that I could have a good reason to divorce her.

But she had been with me for so long, through all of the issues and unfaithfulness that it would be cold-hearted for me to get rid of her out of the blue. The car horn behind me honked, signaling that the light had turned green. I fixed my attention ahead and rolled through the intersection. I couldn't shake the idea that me and Jae would've been perfect together. The way we connected, the way she made me feel and the way I could provide for her. It was all destroyed by a perfect storm of events that neither of us could control.

I rolled to another red light and slowly applied the brakes as I thought about the recording again. I wrecked my mind trying to figure out who could be behind it all. I questioned a few of my maids to see if they had anything to do with it, but they all showed to be innocent with no motive and that made things even more difficult for me to figure out.

I shook my head as the light turned green and drove through the intersection just before I made a right turn. Suddenly, Shayla's image popped in my mind. I hated that she was there at the hospital and she was part of the reason why me and Jae had to end it. Our history was much too strong for Jae to look past. I just didn't think she would still be as crazy over me as to stalk me and track my actions through a new sugar baby.

I gripped the steering wheel just thinking about the fact that she was in the room with Jae arguing with me while she was in the hospital bed. I shook my head and, at that moment, the thought clicked in my mind. I played around with the idea that she could've been the one to plant the recording device in my room, but I didn't give much thought to it until now.

She probably still knew the code to the alarm, so she could've disabled it and come in without setting off any alarms. In addition to that, she knew the way around the bedroom and she could get in there and out without a problem. She was also careless enough to leave the door unlocked on her way out.

She had motive, too. The way things ended between us. The fight between her and my wife in which Carissa was just defending herself because Shayla swung first. I remembered the chaos that ensued after that and the shock that stretched across her face when I told her to leave and that I didn't want anything else to with her. I could tell by the look in her eyes that she wanted to get me back; I just didn't know how or when she would.

From there, I made a U-turn and headed straight for the precinct to let them know that they needed to look at Shayla as a person of interest. I couldn't believe that I didn't think about her before now and since my wife was cleared, the only other person that made sense was her. She had the motive and the means to carry it out and, based on the last conversation we had a few says earlier,

I knew she still wasn't over the drama we had gotten involved in.

As soon as I got to the precinct, I walked into the lobby and asked to speak to the detectives that had been covering my case. I was ordered to have a seat and wait for one of them to come and invite me to the back in their office. Finally, one of them came out front to greet me. I stood up as he extended his hand to me, "Mr. Austin. Hello. Is everything alright?"

I shook his hand. "I think I have somebody you should look at with regards to my case. Another person of interest that just crossed my mind today."

"Oh, really? Alright. Come on back and let's talk about it, because when your wife was cleared of everything, it put is in a tough spot."

"I understand that. I don't know why I didn't think of this person before, but I know she could be good for it."

I followed him down the corridor. A few officers looked my way as we walked by them. I know that my recording was still floating around and because of that, I was still the focus of a lot of attention. I hated it more because Jae was pulled into this web of bullshit and I had to figure out how to end the chapter for the both of us.

I walked into his office and he closed the door behind me, then directed me to sit in the chair on the opposite side of his desk. "So, what do you have for me, Mr. Austin?"

"Her name is Shayla. I used to be involved with her a while ago. She and my wife got into a physical altercation and I had to stand between the two of then to get them to settle down. Anyways, I think she is somebody who could've gotten into my house and set everything off. Planted the camera and everything."

"Are you sure?"

"Yes. She knew the code to my security system. She probably had a key made. I knew I should've changed all those things after we split, but I didn't think she would do something like this. I didn't think she was capable or vindictive enough to try it, but I was wrong. I found out that she was friends with the um—with the woman in the video. She found out that we were seeing each other, and she was jealous."

"How did you find this out?"

"Late last week. We happened to be in the same spot at

the same time and we talked. It was not a coincidence, either. Anyways, I found out that she was still upset about how things happened between us, so, I know she is capable. And she has motive."

"I see." He pulled out a pen a paper. "And what is her name again?"

I told the officer her name. I knew that if they investigated her further, they would possibly find something incriminating to pull her in for questioning. Afterwards, he stood to his feet. "Alright, Mr. Austin. We will look into this person further and see what we come up with. I sincerely hope we find the person behind this all because this invasion of privacy is something that cannot be tolerated. Not at all."

We shook hands and after that, I left the building with the hopes that she would go down for the set up. When I got home, I walked into the bedroom and looked at the area where the camera was positioned in the room. I shook my head, thinking about how she could've come in and slid a camera into position without anyone noticing. I sat down on the bed and exhaled. I had to figure out how to get my life back in line. There was no way that I could bring Jae back into this and I wasn't sure if I wanted to. I wasn't going to leave my wife Carissa and we both knew that. That is, unless she did something that forced me to push her out and I couldn't imagine anything like that happening.

I grabbed my phone and scanned through the pictures of Jae that I couldn't find the courage to delete. I didn't think it would be this hard to move on from her and I never expected my heart to flip for her the way it did. As long as I had been using the sugar baby service, I'd never grown attached to any of the women. Shayla and all of the ones before her were just physical specimens. Women that I used to fill sexual gaps that my wife couldn't.

When I met Jae, it was different. Something about her made me want to give more to her. More of myself, more money. More of everything and I couldn't understand why. It was more than her beauty. It was the way she made me feel. I exhaled and fell backwards on my bed, laying face up at the ceiling. I wanted to call her, but I couldn't bring myself to do it. I didn't want to hear another rejection. Another voice telling me that she didn't want to talk and to stop calling. I had to accept the fact that it was probably best if we both moved on.

I tried to call my wife just to see if she would talk to me, but she forwarded my call as soon as it rang for the first time. I didn't think she would cheat on me while she was out in Belize, but I wouldn't have been surprised if that was what she wanted to do to get back at me. I would've been lying if I said I didn't want to her to do it. Maybe that would be grounds for a divorce and I could get to Jae and live the life that I felt we were supposed to live.

Minutes later, she sent me a text. "I am busy. Will call you later."

I shook my head and leaned back on the bed again. I didn't know what else to do. All I could do was wait on every level. Wait to see if the police would be able to find enough to charge Shayla with the crime, wait to see if Carissa was stepping out on me and also to see if there was still a chance for me and Jae to be together. It was far-fetched, but that was the only thing I could do.

Just then, my phone rang. It was an unknown number and at first, I was opposed to answering it, but on the third ring, I just decided to pick it up. "Hello?" The only thing I heard on the other end was heavy breathing. I sat upright in my bed. "Hello? Who is this?"

The heavy breathing continued as my eyes squinted. I hung up the phone, but it rang just as fast again. "Hello?" The same breathing on the other line. "Listen, I don't have time for these silly little games. If you are a reporter or some other clown trying to get information from me, I will have no problem tracking you down and forwarding the information to the police. So, if you want to continue playing these games, by all means, please do. I have the time and money to handle you accordingly."

"You think I care about your money? About your threats?" The voice was muffled and I could hardly make out what was being said. "I want to see you ruined. I want to see you begging for mercy and I won't stop until that happens. You think that recording was the only thing you were going to have to face? That was just the beginning."

"Listen, I don't—"

A dial tone interrupted my response. At that moment, I knew things were about to get crazier. I just didn't know how fast it was going to happen.

CHAPTER 9

"So, we went to go check out the woman you gave us. We had to go and see what we could find out about her, but it turns out, she has seemingly disappeared."

I sat upright in my chair. The plate of pancakes that my chef prepared was still hot off the skillet. "Disappeared?"

"Yes. We went to her place of residence and she hasn't been there for the past week or so." I thought back to the last time I saw her and that was about a week ago as well. It seemed as if she knew the right time to take off. Like, it was just a matter of time before I connected the dots and had her in the picture for the culprit behind the recording.

He continued, "We went to her employer and checked with a few family members for her whereabouts, but nothing came back. So, we have every reason to believe that she might have something to do with it. We are going to keep digging around to see what we can find."

"Thank you, detective. I appreciate your hard work and diligence. I will do what I can to assist in the investigation. Just call me if I can be of any assistance."

"Will do, Mr. Austin."

I hung up the phone just as my butler poured a glass of orange juice in font of me. I wanted to tell Jae what was going on so she would have a heads up, but I figured it would be best to keep her out of it. She had already been going through enough with the sex tape and I didn't want to make things worse for her. If she wanted to move on, then I had to give her that chance. I could only hope that she would see my commitment to her even though we couldn't get married right now.

I grabbed my phone to make a call to a friend of mine. He was a private investigator and I knew that he could help the police find out where Shayla was at. It wasn't a coincidence that she decided to run away at the same time she popped up on me at the hospital. I was sure she was guilty. Now, I just had to find her and there wasn't a price I wouldn't pay to make that happen.

Jae

"So, what is your experience in this field?"

"I have experience in the customer service field. I've worked in call centers before and I understand what I takes to be successful in this environment and I have the commitment to make it happen."

I sat on the opposite side of her as she scanned through the resume that Angie helped me put together. It was the third interview I'd been on in the last week and I was afraid of being turned away yet again. The woman peered up at me and removed her designer frames. She smiled. We appeared to be around the same age as she placed her glasses on the desk. "I knew I remembered you from somewhere."

My eyebrows scrunched together. "We know each other?"

"Yes. Well, no, we don't know each other, but I know you. I've seen you with um, Mr. Austin? That pretty specimen of a man." I exhaled and shook my head. No matter what I did, or how much time had gone by, I was still remembered as the woman that slept with Blake Austin.

More times than not, I was refused the job because of the attention it would draw to the company or the call center. They didn't want that type of attention and I couldn't blame them, but at the same time, I thought that everyone would have a second chance. Everyone except me. I stood up and draped my purse over my shoulder. "Thank you for your time."

She stood up. "Wait, I am sorry. I hope you don't take this personally, because it is not a personal matter. This is all business and I want you to understand that. I'm sure someone will give you a shot, but unfortunately, it can't be here."

I nodded my head, then exited the room. As I strolled down the hallway, I could feel other people glaring at me on the way out. Even though weeks had gone by, I was still looked at as the same whore on the tape and as of right now, there was nothing I could do about it.

I left the building and walked over to the park nearby, then sat down on the bench in front of a small man-made pond. A duck flapped its wings as it floated on top of the water, then ducked its head into its wing for a few moments. I laughed to myself because I wanted to do the same thing. Disappear for a while and not have to worry about anyone seeing me.

I was still working as a sugar baby because I needed the money, but that was tough because every guy I met wanted to have sex with me. I denied them each time and the next day, I was reassigned with another client. I figured that I would end up getting fired if I kept it up and before now, I thought that would be the best play. Get fired from sugar baby and then I wouldn't have to worry about paying Erica back for anything. But, if I got fired, then I wouldn't have any income, especially since I couldn't find anyone to hire me.

I thought about Kim Kardashian and how she was able to turn her sex tape into a multi-million-dollar industry. She had the know-how, but I didn't know how, and that was the difference between the two of us. Just then, I heard someone walking up behind me. I turned around just in time to see Shayla with a smile on her face. "How was the interview?" she asked

"How did you know I was on an interview?"

"Monica interviewed you, right?" she smiled and sat down beside me on the park bench. "Yes, I know her well. We went to high school together. I told her you would be coming and that you had a um, history, coming along with you."

"You told her about it? About the tape?"

"Well, I didn't have to tell her, Jae," she said, laughing. "That shit was all over the fucking internet. Social media, news stations. Everything. Now, I may have refreshed her memory, but I didn't have to tell her anything."

"Why?"

"My god, are you that dull? Well, I guess you have be if you truly thought we were going to be friends. If you thought we were friends at all. Damn. I would've never thought that you would fall for something so simple. You didn't do your research? You didn't know that I used to fuck around with Blake?"

"If I did, do you think I would've let you befriend me?"

"Shit, hell nah. But, since you gave me the chance, I took it. You know, Blake never did treat me the way he treated you. All this extra shit. Going to the hospital. Going out of the way just to make sure you are ok. I never got any of that and I did far more for his ass than you did, I know that for sure. But, you know how men are. They go after what they think they want, but when they have what they need, they just push it to the side. End up with a bottom ass bitch like you."

"You know what? I don't have time for this bullshit. You want to sabotage my career? My chance to get away from sugar baby and do my own thing? Why? What the hell did I ever do for you to come at me like this?"

"Bitch, you breathed. You fucking spoke to my man and pulled him into some shit that he can't even get out of. You got the fucking treatment that I wanted from him. You did all of that. So, what did you do? You existed. That's it."

I laughed and shook my head. "You are petty as fuck. No wonder why Blake didn't want anything to do with your old raggedy ass. Fuck you, Shayla, and stay the fuck away from me."

"What's wrong, little bitch?" she said as we stood inches away from each other. "You can't handle the fire? Then get the fuck out of the kitchen and go back to the gutters where you belong. You, yo' ratchet ass sister and your dope fiend of an aunt. Fuck all y'all and she can go back to suckin' dick to pay y'all rent you dirty ass bit—"

I balled my fist and struck her across the face. She stumbled backwards in her high heels and then put her hand to her jaw. Her bottom lip trickled blood as she slowly shifted into a smile. "Is that all you got? Shit, you will have to hit me harder than that to keep me away. I will make sure your life is fucking ruined. Trust me, bitch, you will have a hard time doing anything outside of selling pussy to keep yourself from being homeless. I'll chat with you later, sweetheart."

She winked at me and then walked away the same way she came. I wanted to go after her and finish her off because the amount of peace I felt by striking her in the face was something that I needed. I walked to my car, got in and headed back home.

As soon as I got there, I grabbed my laptop and started searching for more jobs. Maybe I had to go a little outside of the city to find one. I knew that the sex tape had become viral, but I had a better chance of moving on in another city as opposed to the one where the scandal took place.

As I scrolled through the job search engine, my phone rang. It was Blake. I sucked my teeth and ignored the call, but just like I suspected, he called right back. I huffed, then grabbed the phone. "What do you want, Blake? I thought I told you not to contact me anymore."

"Yes, you did, but this is about Shayla."

"Shayla? Shit, I don't want to hear nothing else about you or that bitch. Fuck the both of you."

"Wait, Jae, she is the one who recorded our sex tape—"

I stopped with my thumb hoovering above the button to end the call, then slowly moved the phone back to my ear. "She is what?"

"It took me a while to put the pieces of the puzzle together, but, after I spoke to her in the hospital, I slowly started to realize that she was still bitter about how things ended between us. And then, I realized that she still had access to my home. I never changed the codes to the alarm. The locks. Anything. I just figured that she wouldn't try to do anything even remotely similar to what she did a few weeks ago. So, I told the police and they went to track her down, but they can't find her. I hired a private investigator and everything, you know? Because this is serious. I just wanted you to have a heads up about it all so you know to stay away from her."

"Wait." I rubbed my forehead with my thumb and pointer finger. "I just saw her like an hour ago."

"An hour ago?"

"Yes. I had a job interview and she sabotaged it. She told me as much after the fact when I was sitting in the park."

"What park?"

"The one by Convergence. The call center on 123rd."

"Wow. And this was an hour ago?"

"Yes."

"Ok. I'll get this information to my guy. Jae, you need to stay away from her. If she pops up again, call me right away or call the police because they are looking for her. Ok?"

"Yeah. Yeah, alright."

"I need to figure out a way to bring her in for questioning. Are you willing to help?"

"Hell yeah. I'll do whatever I can to help you bring that bitch in."

"Good."

I sat and listened to his plan, hoping that it would work. Maybe if she was arrested, I would be seen as more of a victim than a sex tape star and my life would finally start to return to normal.

CHAPTER 10

I fixed my makeup in the mirror as I got myself ready to go meet with Erica at the sugar baby agency. The plan was in motion. I was supposed to help lure Shayla back out into the open. She seemed to pop up whenever I went out in public, so we both had an idea that she would show up once I went up there to meet with Erica and officially end my contract as a sugar baby.

I lined my lips with lipstick and dabbed my face with foundation. Just enough to cover the small blemishes on my cheek. I hadn't had sex in a while and because of that, tiny pimples came and went over my face. I used a little bit of eyeliner to finish off my eyes and after that, I took a step back and looked at my reflection in the mirror. I had to make sure I was dressed to kill. A sleek cocktail dress that stopped just above my knees and fit every curve on my body.

My hair pulled into a tight ponytail that draped down beyond my shoulders. I winked at myself, and then called Blake to let him know I was ready to head up to the office. "Now, you remember the plan, right? Go in there. Floss what you need to, but don't say a word until Shayla comes. Hopefully, she will show up."

"I'm sure she will. You know how tight she is with Erica. I'm sure she told her that I was coming up there to end my contract with them and she will want to make it into a spectacle."

"Good. So, first you need to stop at the precinct so you can get fitted for the wire."

"A wire?"

"Yes. That is the only way they can record everything. You have to get them talking about it though. Get Shayla to admit that she had something to do with the recording and, after that, we got her. We got her."

I exhaled. I never imagined being so involved in something to the point that I needed to wear a wire just to catch the guilty party, but whatever it was going to take, I was ready. Shayla deserved to be arrested for tying to ruin my life, right along with Blake's. "Alright. I'll head up there before I go to the office. Will you be there?"

"I am already here. Just call me when you arrive and I will meet you outside."

"Ok."

I hung up the phone and then made my way to the precinct. I couldn't wait to get this over with. Too much time had gone by and I was ready to get my lift back and this felt like the first step in the process. I called Blake when I got there and he escorted me in the precinct so they could fit me with the wire. "Are you up for this?" the officer asked as he taped the mic onto me.

"Yes, I am. I am ready to do whatever I need to so that we can get this over with."

"Ok. The most important thing to remember is just to remain natural. Let the conversation come up casually, if possible. After that, they usually will admit whatever they've done on their own. Almost gloating about it, you know? That is normally how we catch our perps when one of our people wears a wire. So, keep that in mind and I'm sure you will get the information we need to put her away."

"Ok, I think I got it. Am I ready to go in?"

The officer stood to his feet. "Yup, you are all set. Speak into the mic for me. I want to make sure the levels are good."

I spoke into the mic and after the sound man gave the thumbs up, we all headed up to the office in different vehicles. My heart thumped inside of my chest the closer we got to the building. I hoped that everything would go the way it was supposed to go and that there would be no problems along with it. Shayla was feisty and I knew it. I also knew that if anybody would gloat about what she did, it would be her.

I pulled up in front of the building and waited a few moments to get the signal that they were ready for me to go in. As soon as I got the signal, I got out of the car and made my way into the building. I pulled the door open and walked up to the lobby on the fourth floor, then waited for Erica to let me know it was time to come in.

I crossed my leg over the other at the knee and bounced my leg up and down, swaying my foot back and forth at the same time. I remembered the first time I came into this place. The nervousness I felt by accepting the job and coaching from Erica. Things started off so well between us, but they quickly soured over time. I though that this job would be able to propel me into other areas and kick start my career. I thought I would make connections by networking with movers and shakers, hopefully opening doors for me further down the line, but now, I realized how completely misguided I was.

This business, although glamourous at times, was not for me and it took a leaked sex tape for me to understand that. Finally, Erica opened the door. She stood in the entryway and smiled, waving me into the office. "Come on in, Jae. I apologize for the wait."

"No problem," I said as I stepped into the office. Sure enough, Shayla was already in there. I stopped in my tracks. "Um, do I need to come back later?" I asked, confused.

"No, you can come in here now and tell Erica why you are too much of a silly, young ass bitch to keep working for us." She tapped the chair beside her. "Come on. Oh, and I just want you to know that the day in the park where you sucker punched me? You won't make it out of this room if you pull that shit again. Consider that your freebie, bitch."

I could tell she was talking shit because her friend Erica was in the room with her. She smiled and sat down behind her desk. "So, from my understanding, you are ready to leave the agency, right?"

"Yes. I have thought long and hard about it and I've come to the conclusion that it is best if I just step away from it all. Things have gone in a totally different direction than I expected before and now, I think it is best that I just give it all up. So," I reached into my pocket and pulled out an envelope full of money. It was reimbursement from all the time, money and effort they spent promoting me on their websites.

Blake gave me every cent of it, and it wasn't a problem for him because it was all chump change in his eyes. Erica looked surprised as I handed her the envelope. "You can count it," I added, "it is all there. Maybe a little extra."

I looked at Shayla. Her top lip curled to the corner of her mouth as she looked surprised. It seemed like she didn't believe that I was able to give back all of the money Erica spent on me. "Now, I think all that is left is the contract. I can sign that and we can be done with this."

Erica counted through the money until she was satisfied, and then got up to retrieve the contract out of her cabinet. "You know, Jae," she said as she plopped it down in front of me, "I had high hopes for you. The day you strolled in here, I looked at Shayla and I said that you were going to be a money maker for this organization. We thought you had what it takes to run the show, but apparently," she threw the pen down on top of the contract, "you were just a fake."

"A fake ass, wanna be boss bitch," Shayla added as she crossed her leg over the other. "You know what? I am glad that that video got released of you. That way, everybody could see how much of a whore you really were. How you step in and steal women's men right from under their nose. You know, that was some of my best work yet."

"Your best work?" I asked with my eyebrows wrinkled together.

"Yes. Some of MY best work. Well, I can't take all of the credit for making that video. I had a little um, inside help, you know? But, I got it done. Shit. I didn't think it would be that easy, either, but when I am dealing with a dumb ass broad like you and a love struck, idiot like Blake, then things become much easier."

I looked at Erica. She didn't say a word as she waited for me to sign the contract. I leaned forward and stroked my signature on the line and afterwards, she quickly snatched it away from me. "Did you know about this?" I asked Erica. Shayla smirked and stifled her laugh before she let it all out. I ignored her. "Did you?"

"I don't know what you are talking about, Jae."

"Don't lie to the bitch," Shayla added, "I can't take all the credit, even if I wanted to." She stood up and slapped five with Erica. "Shit, who can stop us when we get together, huh, Erica? We can ruin a bitch, or a so-called 'un-touchable nigga' like it is nothing."

I shook my head. "Why, Erica? Why?"

"Because, you deserved it, Jae. You came in here thinking you were the hottest thing walking. You were supposed to be bleeding Blake dry just like Shayla was, but you turned out to be a dud. You let your feelings get involved and you practically ruined the best paying client that this organization had. So, I helped plant the recorder. I knew that sex tape would draw attention to my business. One of the best sugar babies I had, and the one of the wealthiest men in the city? A sex tape? Oh, yes. I was going to get all of the attention drawn to this company and, that is what happened. This is business, Jae. Plain and simple. But—" She stood up. "Thank you for your time and your body—because of you, I am sure this business will flourish long after your name is still being dragged through the mud."

In the middle of their laughter, the door popped open and police flooded the room. Erica and Shayla both had looks of horror on their faces as they came in and slapped handcuffs on their wrists. They tried to say a million things a moment, but none of it made sense. They begged to find out what was going on and, before they were both dragged out of the room, I pulled the wire from beneath my dress and flashed it in front of them.

"You bitch!" they both said in sync.

I laughed as they were pulled out of the office, cursing me out with every word in the book. I felt Blake's arm around my shoulder as he breathed a sigh of relief. "Now, I guess we can start the healing process here."

I nodded my head. "Yeah. Yeah, I guess so."

Later that evening, Blake dropped me off at home. He walked me to the door and gave me a hug. "Thanks for everything today. We couldn't have done this without you."

"I am just glad it is over."

"So, where does this leave us now that sugar baby looks like it is about to go down for good?"

"I don't know, Blake. You are still married. I don't know."

Just then, he started moving closer to me for a kiss. I wanted to resist, but I couldn't. I closed my eyes to meet his but right before our lips connected, I heard a familiar voice. A man clearing his throat forced me to open my eyes. Just behind Blake, Darryl stood with his hands in his pockets. "Am I interrupting something?" he asked with a smirk. I couldn't believe he had come back to me. His timing was always something special.

FIND out what happens next in Secrets Of A Sugar Baby Book 4! Available Now!

FOLLOW Mia Black on Instagram for more updates: @authormiablack

SECRETS OF A SUGAR BABY 4

The worst should be over for Jae after the tape scandal and the pain that followed, but unfortunately for her, she's not out of the woods yet. The aftereffects just may be worse than the sin.

She's done with the chaotic life of a sugar baby but figuring out how to regain control of her life, and fixing her relationships with those who suffered because of her choices, will prove to be much more difficult than anything she's ever endured.

With Darryl by her side, it should be easy. That is, if she could get Blake out of her head.

Will she ever get her life back or have things gone too far?

Find out what happens in part four of Secrets Of A Sugar Baby!